The Hitman's Guide to the Galaxy

by Ken Eleson

Published by

1   **halfabook**.com

First Edition July, 2022

The views and opinions contained in this book are not
those of the publisher. This book was published in the
spirit of free thought, that people may continue to think,
grow, discuss ideas, and share the deep thoughts that
form our inner beliefs. We encourage you to exercise free
will, accept whatever truth you choose to believe, but
above all, think and understand.

Manufactured in the United States of America

A Hitman's Guide to the Galaxy
Philosophy
Metaphysics

ISBN 978-1-58884-034-9   (print)
       978-1-58884-035-6   (eBook)

The following is a composition of conversations originally for a podcast on a friend's time finding and working with a "hitter".

1.

"...just for some kind of accounting of the wisdoms and randoms through the whole process. He became my guide to some interesting life lessons and I got to be his guide to a couple cool philosophies of the cosmos."

2.

"If you love someone and they become evil, you should kill them instantly. If you hate someone and they become evil you should let them live a long life. Sounds backwards until you unpack it. His reasoning in this line is based on the idea that we have an immortal soul. This soul will suffer less in the afterlife if you don't allow it the time to twist itself beyond repair with evil deeds. If you let a person go on ruining their soul, they will suffer longer and perhaps eternally in the afterlife."

3.

"It's always night time. The main star comes into view and lights up life for us, but our true existence is what we see at night. The planet as a whole lives in the blackness of space. When you feel that, it gives a deep comfort to night time. Usually we feel safer and more confident during the light of day and our insecurities and fears classically come out when it's dark. With enough coaching of the idea you begin to see that daytime still is night time and there's no emotional swing with the light. It all becomes the same, it's always night time.

4.

"My plan to find a hitter was to move the wrong kind of drugs with the wrong kind of people hoping that eventually I would meet the right man."

5.

"...had a connection through an older friend who was a capable manufacturer outside of San Francisco. I went to visit him knowing he had the highest quality stuff and made quite a large purchase. He gave me a couple pieces of advice on selling the stuff and I told him I was just planning on giving it all away."

6.

"...coming around to the holidays just before Halloween and I started getting into it. There would be some colorful parties to show up at and people would be ready to play."

7.

"...on Halloween night sitting next to a guy I hadn't seen for a while. He didn't recognize me because of my mask so I kept messing with him asking odd questions and stuff. Eventually the lady I was with told him who I was and ruined the joke but it made a good connection."

8.

"...not a really important part, and it's kinda embarrassing. Just a mask."

9.

"...a couple quick jumps after the Halloween night connection and I was with a high school friend Kara who had married into the world of the nightlife. It was through her that I got invited to a poker night which I'd heard was a deeper scene."

10.

"...would bring her a bottle of wine or champagne and we would sit off to the side at an island bar looking over the poker game. Over a few weeks of conversation she gave me a good idea of who each person was. The table was actually two tables and almost 20 players. I knew nothing about playing cards but soon I was at the table losing money every Friday just listening. I first learned that it was a blend of watching the cards, thinking of positions in the betting rotation, seeing reactions to the money, calculating odds. Then a guy told me to stop watching the cards and money and just watch everyone else watching the cards and money. Looking more closely at him I noticed his eyeglass frames were jeweled."

11.

"By chance he was from San Antonio and that spiked the whole thing. It's always a meeting of minds when you understand the same organization."

12.

"...moved into Foosball and he came over saying he was good on defense asking to double the game. I joked with him about how he'd better be ready to kick some ass because I'd developed a reputation to uphold. His response was "Alright I like that."

13.

"...joking our way through some of the nice shots and blunders I finally asked him if he had any interest in some high quality exotic stuff. He said "Always." When I brought it out he was confused and thought I was talking about marijuana not MDMA etc. He said he wasn't much into it himself because he worried about the quality. I assured him what I had was as good as it gets, and it was, so he had his girlfriend come over and take a look at it. She made a comment that what I had was "special" and that was all the blessing it needed."

14.

"...hell of an evening out of Foosball."

15.

"...generosity and humor I quickly had myself into a new life. I started going over to his place to watch games and hang out for barbecues. I always brought popular things to share with his guests and it wasn't long before I was fully accepted and even expected to be there. Of all things the guy was a truly great host and had dozens of interesting friends in and out each week."

16.

"...help of Thanksgiving, Christmas, and New Year's Eve things moved quickly."

17.

"...started a new relationship with a lady I met at a party and accepted myself as a new person."

18.

"...yea, butterfly painted on her face,
barefoot in a dress playing volleyball, and
just killin' it."

19.

"...got comfortable in this circle, I began to zero in on another guy who I felt could be the next step to the connection I was looking for. He moved through easily and confidently, had been involved with local level hustles, and I'd heard rumors that he was the one who shot someone in a nearby convenience store several years ago. He was also pretty good at chess and that became a bit of a dynamic with us."

20.

"...introduced me to some new music and a slightly different scene. A little more "live for the moment" type. Some beautiful humans."

21.

"...felt they were chasing something. Not quite there and always moving on. Just a different feeling to the whole scene. Like none of them expected to live long enough for any long term plans to matter."

22.

"...feeling good about how everything was going until my ex-girlfriend called one morning. She had a dream about me being surrounded by people in "black military style gear" closing in on my old house. She said it was "like a swat team or FBI" coming to get me and she needed to warn me about it. Her phone call slowed things down a bit."

23.

"...little over a year of living a new life and even finding myself very much in love with the lady I was with, I finally felt ready one evening to bring up the topic of looking for a hitter with my chess partner. He was setting up some turntables for a friend's house party and I walked up with "So I kinda need to chat about something goofy." I remember saying the word "goofy" and him noticing that this was going to be a bit out of the ordinary."

24.

"By the end of the evening I had said what I'd waited so long to say and it didn't phase him at all. Not that he was expecting it, but he wasn't surprised."

25.

"...insisting he accept some kind of finder's fee and he said he liked a pair of special release Nike shoes that had just come out at around $250. He again made it clear there was no guarantee that I could actually meet with the hitter and beyond that there was no guarantee the guy would actually work with me. I didn't care and dove right in."

26.

"...brought over a bag of silver coins which were quarters of a wide range of the silver minting years to pay for the connection. The quarters had come from a trade years ago and had just been sitting because I was hoping they would someday skyrocket in value. That skyrocket never launched. We used a scale with MDMA drifting around on it to count out roughly $1500 in the day's silver market price per ounce. I also assumed they'd be valued differently as quarters and said I wasn't exactly sure what they were worth. Counting through them I liked the look and feel of the much older coins which were smoothed and thinner with a dark patina. The newer years had thick edges and engravings, nice and bright, and noticeably heavier but I liked the older ones and kept those, about $300 worth by weight, giving him the rest. I enjoyed the fact that I was paying with silver coins."

27.

"I had become delusional enough to think this was proper, silver coins are how you're supposed to pay for dealings in death right?"

28.

"He got the shoes, I got a meeting with a man who had almost a dozen paid kills."

29.

"...an odd relationship with shoes now. I'll take them off and walk away from them. I left a pair at a crosswalk and just crossed the street recently, those were pretty new. Then I left the next pair at a bench after sitting down for a minute. Had those only a few days. Mostly it's not an issue and I just kinda go through the world in socks."

30.

"...wanted to meet where I liked to practice handball and felt more comfortable than just about anywhere else in the city. I also knew this was usually a very dead empty place where you could see anyone around from a good distance. I had my headphones on listening to 1967 Ravi Shankar playing live at the Monterey International Pop Festival. I always liked the 27 minute Raga Bhimpalasi track while playing handball. For some reason this helped me move correctly on the ball and around the court. I was able to feel the difference in those moments where I should hang back letting the ball develop off the wall, and when I should rush in and attack it before it developed too much. This Ravi track and handball became a regular meditation for me and I felt comfortable in the headphones. As he approached me I kept tossing the ball against the wall trying to be casual. He got closer, I took the headphones down to hang around my neck, took off my glove and said "good evening" reaching to shake his hand. He shook my hand and nodded at me 'good evening'."

31.

"Him being younger than me shocked me. For some reason I just wasn't expecting that. I had just hit 24 and he was going 21/22. We talked briefly about our common friend and joked that he was the true wild-card among any of us. He asked about a couple other people I might know which I did and that certainly helped us get some trust with each other. Eventually he got into a quick list of seemingly standard questions. I just kept throwing the ball at the wall, sometimes bouncing it off the ground in front of me and letting my mind race. He wanted to walk a bit and from there we went through a couple baseball fields and ended up in a neighborhood sitting in a small cement gazebo type structure. We didn't say much for a while after first sitting, just watched a couple locals walk their dogs and listened to some kids riding bikes up and down the street."

32.

"...Lewis style savior structure highlights the understanding and forgiveness. If we make a minor mistake it's easy to recognize it and apologize. The bigger our faults, the more difficult they are to accept as our fault. We want to see and say where it's maybe only half our fault due to other peoples' behavior or just the situation itself that caused the problem. If we do something really terrible we distance ourselves further from responsibility and say it's completely the fault of the situation or other people. It takes a really good person to admit to a horrible fault, but a really good person usually isn't going to have horrible faults. So we have a situation where good people are good at atonement but don't need it much, and bad people are bad at atonement but need a lot of it. The worse you are, the better you have to be. This is where a forgiving savior really helps. God forgives us, and that feels great. Then we realize it feels great because we know we have things to be forgiven for. Rather than start the atonement process with admitting our terrible deeds, we start with forgiveness and then go back."

33.

"I was looking pretty intently at the moon. The sky was shifting blue to black and it was glowing nicely. He noticed this, kinda made fun of me about it and then asked."

34.

"...just finished working with a local company that built a large light collector to concentrate a beam of moonlight to be as bright as the Sun. The device was about 3,000 square feet of mirrored panels the size of doors mounted up in the air on a hydraulic rotate and tilt system. Each panel was slightly concave so that the whole structure came together like the inside of a large mirrored sphere. With some practice we could track the moon's path through the sky and keep a concentrated beam. There is no radiation and no UV in the moonlight and the lunar light affects the biorhythms of nearly all life on Earth. The idea behind the company was that moonlight was healing by resetting our overall energy into balance."

35.

"...he was explaining how the moon has a symbolic understanding of the changes that we go through as people. We know feelings of growing and diminishing, we know being full and being empty, and the moon as our dear friend knows these as well. He kept talking about the feeling of it being so close to us. Far enough away that we can escape the problems of the Earth, but close enough that we can always come right back."

36.

"...traveling between worlds as a feeling from his childhood. Originally he was from Peru. Then went to Australia to live with an aunt where he first learned English. From there he ended up in Mexico then back and forth across the line with our state. It wasn't something I noticed beforehand but afterwards I could hear the slight Aussie accent on some of his words. Not something I'd ever really thought about in the world."

37.

"...on a hill in a boom looking into this beam with a radio to inform coworkers which way to move the mirrors. We did this regularly because the wind was able to move the whole structure sometimes and cause small tweaks in the imaging on each mirror. They put water in the moonlight to see how it restructured the molecules, grew sprouts and analyzed their mineral content, people wanted to bathe in the moonlight, including Dr. Emoto who sang some opera in the beam I think?"

38.

"...clocked far more time in this beam of light than anyone and in doing so became the most moonlight exposed human to ever live."

39.

"...he's joking about if that meant supervillain or superhero. We figured a guy in a concentrated beam of Sun had it worse and became the villain so I get to be the hero."

40.

"...don't know who's to say but I can be super calm. At the same time I'm premium crazy. I guess that's the Lunatic part of the whole moonlight thing."

41.

"..talked about the many worlds analysis in physics. Went into the plurality of worlds in philosophy, and from there things got crazy. There's no way out, we live in an awesome reality."

42.

"...not that we really collapse the waves. We don't actually collapse a superposition of both 'dead' and 'alive'. Instead we understand ourselves as quantum creatures existing in one world among multiple worlds. There's a world that sees the cat alive, then sees me open the box and see the cat alive, and another world that sees the cat dead, then sees me open the box and see the cat dead. Two different worlds completely. So we're becoming entangled with the superpositions, not collapsing them. The wave is what's real. The collapse of the wave is a limited perception."

43.

"...could say many things about him but they're all non-rigid designators of his identity. We can say he's the guy with a beard, is married to Sharon, won the tennis tournament etc. but all of these are just possibilities, they're not necessary. He could exist without a beard, marry a different lady named Rachel, lose the tennis tournament and he's still him. Now his existence is also just a possibility. We don't want to say his existence is necessary, like he's a necessary universal being. Once he's here standing in front of us though, it's odd to say his existence is just possible. What's housing the possibility of his non-existence when he's standing here? Another world, world W prime where he doesn't exist. The sum total of worlds allows for his existence and non-existence so we don't end up saying ridiculous things about the necessity of his existence."

44.

"... that we were similar in personality, but clearly from very different worlds."

45.

"...only other thing I'd ever really done was sneak into an amusement park at night and climb a roller coaster with my best friend. We got caught on the way down and I didn't have ID so I went to jail until they could prove who I was."

46.

"...involved researching habits and routines to find the right method and moment to deliver a dose of cyanide or something of similar effect. Much later I learned about a couple very clever delivery methods. "

47.

"...not something I'll be saying much at all about. We all know humans are awesome and they can get really creative."

48.

"...will say is that after the research is done to design the right moment, it's all about the paths in and out. Everything is timing and movement."

49.

"...ability to have an effect on the moment is just as much a technology as anything else. Really you don't need to even touch anything because you're already connected to it."

50.

"...planet is almost a closed energetic system but the sunlight is the cleansing new energy. Then there's the energy of the moonlight, and the tiny bits from the distant stars."

51.

"...didn't agree on anything officially that first night. It seemed he just wanted to get a read on my level of sincerity in wanting a person off the planet. I told him about the Socratic philosophy of killing those you love if they become evil and letting your enemies go on twisting their souls which certainly grabbed his interest.

52.

"...explained that the man I wanted to hit had become lost in the world and was beyond bringing back, he was only going to get worse. Taking him off the planet was "non-optional", and I simply had to do it."

53.

"...him telling me to think about it and really decide if this was worth the risk. His initial advice was to let it go and forget about all the things the world has going on. Of course I didn't take his advice."

54.

"Driving home that night was just surreal.
Absolute other world."

55.

"...second meeting was interesting. I could tell by how he was looking at me that I had become a real curiosity for him."

56.

"...insisted we sit inside his car with no cell phones and anything logistical or of any consequence we'd write on a piece of paper on the center console instead of saying out loud. When we were finished he folded and shredded the paper like big confetti then shoved the shreds inside a Gatorade bottle with some water, several minutes later he shook it into a pulp. He said there was definitely no one around but in theory a distance microphone like they use on football fields makes paper notes to burn or pulp a good habit. We agreed on a price which I thought was frighteningly inexpensive and he had simple instructions to pay someone else after everything was done and he'd gone back to Mexico."

57.

"...watching a local pick up game and the conversation led to me unpacking some of my deeper mind. I noticed right away he was very engaged in what I was saying. It sounded ridiculous, and I'm sure it was mostly a joke, but at the end of it he said "between the two of us, you're the one who's truly terrifying."

58.

"...due to my passion for a reality based on the teachings of Krishna in the Bhagavad Gita which I constantly referenced that night."

59.

"...brings a powerful philosophy of morality to the concepts of Selfhood, death, and duty. It was a book I'd been familiar with through my parents' professional involvement in Yoga, and it took over my life in this situation."

60.

"...main figure of the Gita is the warrior prince Arjuna who finds himself on the battlefield in a civil war against his uncle and cousins for control of the Indian empire. Arjuna's older brother was too young for the crown at the time of their father's death, so control of the empire went to their uncle who was to rule until the boy came of age. When the time came to give the empire back their uncle and cousins decided they'd rather keep the crown."

61.

"...day of the great battle Arjuna is ready to kill any and all who have come to challenge him. He proudly commands his charioteer to drive him down the battle line so that he may gaze into the eyes of the men who have come to die at his hand. Well known to be one of the most deadly warriors on either side of the battle, he wants to remind everyone of just who they're messing with."

62.

"...rolling down the battle line looking into their faces, he is reminded that he knows most of them all too well. They are his own people. Uncles, cousins, grandfathers, brothers, sons, brothers-in-law, sons-in-law, elders, his friends, old schoolmates, former teammates and coaches, his old archery master who first taught him the bow etc.

Seeing the reality of having to kill his own people to win the empire his mind begins to spiral. His mouth goes dry, his skin grows hot, his breathing becomes erratic and the very life within him begins to leave him faint. His grip on his magical bow Gandiva (given to him by the god of thunder) slips in his hand and his legs no longer have the strength to hold him.

He calls to his charioteer in distress saying this isn't worth it. He's not interested in killing them even if it won him all of Heaven, much less an Earthly Kingdom. He says even if they've come to fight out of some ignorance and they're in the wrong, shouldn't

he with his sight of the higher truths refuse
to engage them in their own violence?"

63.

"Let not their wrath be our wrath? Let not their guilt be our guilt? He throws his bow into the sand and says "I will not fight"."

64.

"Both armies watch as Arjuna is crushed by this moment of grief."

The response he gets from his driver and lifelong friend changes his life and changed mine as well."

65.

"Arjuna's compassion for the men of the battlefield is commendable, but he has misunderstood the reality he lives in."

Your grief is for nothing!
Do not mourn for the living or the dead!

What is
never ceases to be !

Let them perish, Prince! Fight!
Birthless and deathless and changeless
remaineth the spirit forever;
Death cannot touch it at all!

Arjuna may kill the minds and bodies of these assembled warriors, but the true Divine Self, which is the real Self cannot die. The Self cannot be wetted by water, burned by fire, is unborn, uncreated, un-caused, un-analyzable, and ultimately, un-killable.

There are no qualities that can be attached to it. The Divine Self is untouchable by any conceptualization of its nature."

66.

"Krishna also teaches that because Arjuna is a member of the Kshatriya (warrior) class, his duty is to fight on the battlefield for his family and his empire.

Interestingly, with Krishna there is no universal set of commandments regarding sin. Instead, there is only your path and your duty to your path. Each of us has God given talents and experiences and we have a duty to these talents and experiences.

We only sin if we ignore our path or try to walk another's path.

The warrior must not walk off the battlefield to write poetry, and the poet must not drop his pen to pick up a bow.

There is no way out. Krishna's eventual message to the warrior prince is "Pick up your bow and fight!"

"My new friend with a lifetime of kills to his name was just as fascinated with this philosophy as I was.

67.

"Krishna blesses the warrior prince with divine vision and reveals himself in stunning fashion, Lord of the Universe and all that exists within it, he wears our whole cosmos like a necklace of jewels."

Krishna is endless life, boundless love, bitter death and joyous birth.

Unborn, undying, un-begun.

Blazing, glowing, flashing and spinning. Turning darkness to dazzling day with a gaze.

Eyes of fire, consuming all.

Reducing the soldiers of the battlefield into dust.

Creating and destroying creatures infinitely.

68.

"Arjuna is overwhelmed by this sight.
Krishna explains to him,

Thou seest me as Time.

Who kills.

Time who brings all to doom.
The Slayer Time, Ancient of Days, come
hither to consume;
Excepting thee, there stands not one shall
leave the battlefield alive!

Arise! obtain renown! destroy thy foes!
Fight for the kingdom.
By Me they fall- not thee!

My instrument art thou!
Strike, strong-armed Prince strike!

Deal death.

'Tis I who bid them perish! Thou wilt but slay
the slain!

69.

"We are to understand that this experience is granted to Arjuna not by wisdom, not by sacrifices or alms, not by works well done, nor penance or prayers or reciting psalms. The vision was granted because Arjuna's heart had been shaken, he was truly suffering and found himself in perfect faith and uttermost surrender. Krishna returns to his human form, Arjuna's mind is able to think again, his heart beats steadily. Only when Krishna sees us with our hearts truly open does he know we have attained the position to truly understand."

70.

"He said he'd experienced that moment, and it had the feeling his grandmother was involved in helping him."

71.

"...talked about the different ways it could work that grandmothers can help us from the beyond. It seems alien, but it's technology we haven't unpacked yet. He thought it could be something like a postcard left behind by his grandmother at her point of death. The spirit has moved on but in the moment of death the scope of the person is such that we can leave messages and occurrences for others. This was his theory based on how it felt to him. It was like a gift that was left for him but she wasn't actually there to talk to."

72.

"...human mind can kind of imagine the cessation or absence of Time but not really. We just imagine everything stopping its motion. All the material freezes in place, but the clock keeps going. We would say "Wow time stopped for almost 5 minutes" type nonsense. But we really can't even begin to imagine the cessation or absence of space. We can play with the magnitude of space by shrinking the whole universe down to a dot, but we still imagine that dot is floating 'somewhere'. If we imagine blowing the whole cosmos apart into vanishing bits we're still thinking about the empty 'space' left behind. Or the classic "beyond the edge of the universe?". We can picture some kind of void space or 'different' space but not Non-space, what the hell is Non-space?"

73.

"...so we see that space is not a concept created by our minds. It's the inextricable framework for any cognitive experience. There are no thoughts or experiences of pure reality. Everything we 'know' is based in relationships of cognitive conceptualizations. Reality is not a concept and cannot be conceptualized, it's impossible to 'know' anything about it."

74.

"...a kind of morality in each breath. We put our energy signature into everything. The atoms we're breathing in and then releasing become coded in a way. We have a duty to take a breath with an understanding that it literally is the shared spirit of the air and oceans. Be happy to be alive and sharing it. When we die too we want to leave behind a body with good code on the atoms for the worms and mushrooms to eat, the plants to eat, the deer to eat, for us to again eat the deer. It's just constant recycling of the atoms so we want to make sure we're putting a good signature on everything. I think that was Epicurus?"

75.

"...walking back to our vehicles, we ended that evening with an odd exchange of looks. I smiled, chewing my lips in some sort of an apology or embarrassment for how crazy I must seem, and he looked at me with raised eyebrows that seemed to say "Yea you're crazy".

76.

"Eventually we were hanging out maybe weekly and then more. I bought him a pair of good handball gloves and convinced him to play, we jumped in here and there at the basketball courts, went to parties and leaned against backyard walls watching the show..."

77.

"...much like how someone changes in your eyes when you see them do something they're really good at. It kinda makes them more attractive or interesting. You can only see them if they show you themselves."

78.

"...letting the air rip through and the odometer passed about 135. Looking through the moon roof to the stars it felt like cruising under the ocean."

79.

"...passion for rooftops and he always wanted to drop something, usually something glass. Most often this was one of those apple shaped Martinelli's juice bottles but also anything that might fall or float in an interesting way or make a cool sound when hitting the ground. Pocket change is a bit of fun to rain into the concrete, and I learned that those little plastic coffee creamers make a nice pop when they hit. One of the more big ticket items for him was a wide oval table top basically like a small surfboard that he thought he would get to land right on its edge..."

80.

"...up on the first one it makes it easier to get onto the next one. Going from rooftop to rooftop was usually just a slight level change up or down and you're all the way down the road."

81.

"...walking through every little area and becoming familiar with the side streets and behind all the buildings. Made it very different to drive past those places again. You really know where you are once you've walked through it all."

82.

"...was the calmest side of the road tire change I've witnessed. He just wasn't bothered by any of it. It didn't even interrupt our conversation. Like it was just as ordinary as needing to pull over for fuel."

83.

"Weapons are much better suited for escape rather than attack. It would take a very brave, confident, or I suppose crazy, person to come at you while you're holding a knife and this is especially true of pistols. If you're using a pistol to try to go through someone you will most likely have to actually shoot them. If your only goal is to escape you can simply point it at them and walk backwards. Continuing this theory, if you have six shots in a pistol then you can only go through six people and that's assuming you're hitting your mark each time, which is difficult even if you're well trained. You can escape from sixty people though by simply aiming the pistol while walking away. If you walk a precise path keeping your footwork and aim correct you could theoretically get away from any number of people without firing a single shot.

Picture yourself in the grocery store and everyone wants to kick your ass for some reason. Unless they're willing to give up their lives for a chance at landing a good punch you could carefully navigate your way around and through the aisles to get out the front door by keeping good movement. This wouldn't work if they were all zombies, but any life-loving human you aimed at would either stop in their tracks or run away. You could find your way out the door into the parking lot and into your car without pulling the trigger."

84.

"...let a situation develop itself in whatever direction. This couple mistook him for an employee at the store and he plays along helping them find the Greek olives they were looking for and he apologized for not having the back-stock pulled to the front of the shelf. He also thought pretending we were a couple to see what reaction he could get out of people was a good one."

85.

"...never heard anyone's last words or stood there for someone's last breath."

86.

"...was a happy person like the rest of us and I'm sure he slept well most nights. There were also days he was a little more gone."

87.

"...belief in it. Made each moment happen with just that. Because the possibility is there. It's real. Just cruise through and be in it, be there to guide it in. Open the spacetime for it. Call it in. Then guide it in."

88.

"...far more time thinking about their kids than thinking about them. What does the world look like for the little guys who lose their..."

89.

"...and the way he put it was just "You're the hitters". So I know he found a certain amount of self forgiveness in recognizing that none of what he did was really him. These are our problems."

90.

"...never really felt home. Both our apartments were empty like no one lived there. At one point I hadn't been back to my place for almost three months. We like to think we do it because we're exploring. It's just escaping."

91.

"...only after I noticed his driver's seat had the buckle clicked together with no belt on it. He had gone to a scrap yard and cut a seatbelt just to take the buckle. This way he could leave it always clicked together to keep the vehicle's warning chime from constantly ringing without actually having to wear the belt. This was the second vehicle he'd done this to. He thought of it like an offering, like if God wanted an easy way to take him."

92.

"...similar to your local doctor giving advice on healthy living habits so you don't need to visit the clinic. It would be a show about his advice on how to never need your local hitter. Focus on loving your kids, don't get involved in dirty business, keeping good friends, choosing an honest wife. Perfect ongoing joke..."

93.

"...been up all night with some kind of fever and had this song stuck in my head not letting me sleep. I told him about it earlier that day. Then I was finally feeling better that evening playing pool at a lady's birthday, or maybe it was her graduation, but he goes over and puts the damn song on the jukebox with a cartoon smile."

94.

"...fun of him at one point for his analysis on two brands of orange soda. He said one of them kept the flavor of the real juice, wasn't over sweetened and had the right amount of carbonation, and the other one was "trying too hard". He also had an opinion on every new kind of chips or re-make of a Reese's, all of that. Just constant. The best pizza depending on preferred crust style and toppings, the "correct" Al Pastor, the "cleanest" Lo Mein..."

95.

"...on how love is greatest when it's friends with great trust. Imagine two men on the battlefield who both trust each other with their lives and more importantly with the aftermath of their deaths. When it's taken out of the context of romance or attraction it hits something higher."

96.

"...not the best idea to be walking around with a pistol if you're trying to keep anyone from thinking anything of you, but carrying a knife is common enough and when used properly a blade can be a much faster and sure way to defend yourself. In close range you can quickly end up tangled fighting for your grip on a pistol. Assuming you do pull a pistol out in time you will also have to hit your target quickly and in the right spot to really stop them or they'll rush into you. He was a firm believer in a fixed blade knife and using the downward grip in the rear hand. The disadvantage to the forward style in the front hand is that if you lunge or stab at someone and miss they can grab your arm or wrist and you'll be fighting for control of the blade. If the blade is oriented downward it cuts right into a hand grabbing under your wrist and a quick roll of the wrist pushes the blade into their forearm if they're grabbing from the topside."

"...blade upright also becomes dangerous if your elbow folds in because the point is then coming right at your own face and chest. With the point downward your elbow can fold in and the knife is still pointed outward at your opponent. This is important if you're up close with the other person and especially if you fall with them on top of you. You want your blade directed at your opponent's face and chest rather than have it coming into your chest. Finally, the downward grip uses the strength of your index and middle fingers rather than pushing the butt of the knife out through your pinky and ring finger. This may all be difficult to visualize but if you pick up a blade and try it you will easily see what I mean. We practiced with sharpie markers just to demonstrate how messy and difficult it is to attack someone with a blade. It's very difficult to take a knife away in any case without being marked up with sharpie lines enough to be in critical condition. Keeping the blade in the rear hand also allows you to use your forward hand to jab and push away attacks for a good set up shot. After some decent practice I had enough confidence with a knife that I felt it would take three people to get the blade out of my hand."

97.

"... key part of secrets is not using drugs or alcohol. Getting drunk easily leads to not caring about consequences and pairing this with feelings of closeness or friendship can easily let words fall out of your mouth. I never really developed a relationship with alcohol so that wasn't much of an issue, but other drugs had been a part of my recreational life and I was advised to cut their use to an extreme minimum if I couldn't bring myself to quit entirely. I did well for the most part but did end up smoking herb here and there and using some hallucinogens in moments where I really needed to live in a different reality. Most often if I did use drugs I was alone out in the desert talking to the moon and stars and not about anything to do with the hit."

98.

"...good listening because people are always saying more than they realize. At one point I had invested in some gemstones with a "friend of a friend" and due to miscalculated weights by the seller we ended up with more stones than we'd paid for. The seller realized this mistake several days later and called asking us to bring some of the stones back. This was a bit of a big deal because we traveled from the southwest U.S. to Nova Scotia to meet for the purchase. The other guy was unwilling to go back or give anything back and considered it the seller's problem that we ended up with more than we'd paid for. I called the seller and said I would return with my portion of stones and give back whatever was over my half. I traveled all the way back to Nova Scotia just to do this.

When the guy picked me up from the airport everything was normal, he was the same nice guy I'd met when we did the original purchase. At one point during the drive he brought up the Bible doubting whether it was all real, whether Jesus ever existed as a historical figure type stuff. I entertained the conversation as I usually enjoy hearing peoples' opinions and criticisms. When we got back to his place and started going through the stones it was obvious I actually did have far too much for what we had paid. He made a quick move with the pile, shoved them in his safe and closed it locked. He was upset that my "friend" refused to bring anything back and took all of what I had so I'd take all of what the other guy had as punishment. Driving back to the airport he began to feel his guilt hit hard and kept apologizing and asking me to forgive him. He pulled over to puke on the side of the highway and was in a state of panic over what he had done. I got what I needed out of the guy with the other half of the stones by giving him a minor heart attack over the phone, actually ended up in the hospital. He mailed me a package and I eventually moved on. Still, if I'd been listening during the drive in Nova Scotia, I would have had a different ride."

99.

"...something to be said for Arjuna's uncle in challenging his nephews for control of the empire. If he does this consciously, knowing they will better serve the empire after having to fight for it rather than just inheriting it, then he knows his purpose and serves it.

This is similar to the Joker testing and refining Batman. He really wants to see that Gotham is protected by the best version of Batman possible, so he's willing to be the one to test him to his limits. Lex luthor too.

Valuable villain because he's trying to demonstrate to humanity that we don't need some super-powered alien to be solving all of our problems. We can create our own flying suits with super strength and use laser blasters if we need to."

100.

"...who the coolest guy to ever live is, and he wears a pink Carnation. We follow Charlie as he arrives on a boat in Antwerp to meet his wife at a hotel. He shows up much later than expected and heads to the hotel room where he finds the doors unlocked and his wife already in bed asleep. As he's changing clothes and climbing into bed with her he hears someone trying to open the door and goes to see who it is. He opens the door to a very well dressed young man wearing a pink Carnation in the button of his jacket.

"What struck Charlie the moment he looked at him was the expression in the young man's face. It was so radiant with happiness, it shone with such gentle, humble, wild, laughing rapture that Charlie had never seen the like of it. An angelic messenger straight from Heaven could not have displayed a more exuberant, glorious ecstasy."

The young man at first seems bewildered then says, "I beg your pardon. I infinitely regret to have disturbed you." and goes off happily down the hallway.

Charlie begins to question this encounter thinking that perhaps his wife had met this man in the hotel and invited him to her room since he had not arrived. He gets out of bed disturbed with this thought and goes out into the town to do some thinking. As the morning comes around he returns to the hotel and finds his wife awake downstairs at the hotel cafe having coffee. When they go back up to their room Charlie notices that it's not the same room he was in last night. He further realizes he must have actually been in the young man with the Carnation's room, with *his* lady and the guy was just too high on life to let it bother him."

101.

"...was a feeling like I could do anything and I just went for it, whatever was going on. Had a bunch of 'lucky' wins on the chessboard and really got surgical with the timing playing handball."

102.

"...started playing piano from some tutorials online. Mostly songs from a movie my lady was really into, but I got pretty good at it."

103.

"...bought canvases and color and started
painting which I'd never done. They were
bad at first but soon I was doing these Birger
Sandzen meets Yvonne Jaquette style
cityscapes that were cool."

104.

"...called me the day his lady decided she wouldn't be going through with a pregnancy. I met her a few times and knew he didn't share much info with her but she knew enough. We met to take a walk and just talk but he didn't make it very far. Just sat on the ground at the perimeter of the parking lot we met in and cried. For most of the conversation he didn't make eye contact and just looked at the ground. I remember one moment of him looking me directly in the eyes with tears saying just one line about her. It was awesome the way he loved her."

105.

"...blamed himself for her decision, blamed himself for all of his decisions and the person that he'd become in life. I listened to him rapidly calculating different versions of his past and himself that might've led to a different outcome."

106.

"...conversations here and there about methods I decided I wanted to do the hit myself. For weeks he insisted against it, telling me to think about my family and the risk I was already taking. At this point I didn't have a child so it was harder for me to anchor myself into the world and think about real consequences. I told him in a worst-case scenario I would disappear from the USA into Mexico then into South America. Maybe someday I'd come back. I'd also been to south China and picked up the language decently. I thought I could get back there and be in another world entirely. "

107.

"...take some time off to think about it, and I agreed but my mind was made up just as it had been after our first meeting. In the time I took to "think about it" I built two silencers and pictured myself ending a man's life with a pistol I named Gandiva after Arjuna's bow."

108.

"...first silencer was built from a machined piece that was ordinary enough that it could have been for several different uses and I felt safe buying it from a fabricator in a nearby small town. When I went to the counter, I made a big mistake. The man put an invoice across the table asking me to sign for the pickup and I hesitated. He noticed something wasn't right as I paused looking at the paper. He says "Doesn't have to be your name, just put a name on it." I signed it, he looked at me sincerely and said "Good luck".

109.

"Looking back, that was a horrible error."

110.

"...fired a couple shots through that one and was really disappointed. It worked, but not well enough."

111.

"We all experience the hijacking of our rationality by our emotionality."

112.

"We fight with the people we love, we make extravagant
purchases, we overeat candies, we throw and break things. Ultimately we become separated from
the wisdom of our spiritual selves when emotions collapse our rationality.
In early Eden rationality, emotionality, and spirituality are in harmony as Adam, Eve, and God.
Maintaining this harmony relies on a single specific rule. Eve and Adam are not to
eat from the Tree of Knowledge of Good and Evil.
Our spirituality is the only one capable of knowing the difference between good and evil.

In the classic lesson from the garden of Eden our emotionality, Eve, eats from the
tree first, then brings the fruit back to our rationality, Adam, and they both fall from harmony. We are all very familiar with this process in the mind. Our emotions

believe they 'know' something to be 'good' or not and tangle our
rationality in the net.
Our emotions are well suited to guide us in many ways, and our rationality is obviously a powerful tool in making judgments. It is only the specific domain of "knowledge of good and evil" in which they cannot be trusted.
The true crux of this disharmony process is not our emotions, it is the snake. This snake happens to be well named by Indian philosophers as Ahamkara, the "I-Maker" in our consciousness.
The snake poisons the mind with an "I" which believes itself to be separate from
the interconnected cosmos of atoms that compose our reality.
Having a feeling of separation, an "I" which stands separate from all else is the
true cause of our downfall.
Living separate from the cosmos is impossible.
God had said Eve and Adam would die if they ate from the Tree of Knowledge of
Good and Evil.
Death here is a spiritual death as we become disconnected with our spiritual self.

113.

"...second silencer was a simple modification of a high quality multi-walled thermos with some 'wipes' installed. I had more confidence in the second try. It worked much better and I was pretty proud of myself but nowhere near canceling the sound like we've seen in movies. I decided a pistol would not be my method. I had no experience with explosives, and they seemed too traceable, so I found myself agreeing with a poison and started thinking about a good delivery moment and method.

114.

"...had it in the backpack and she went looking for the keys. She had the piece out asking me what the hell it was but she knew. I tried to lie and say I was just playing around, I thought it would be fun to try building a silencer kind of thing. Of course that didn't work and she pretty well demanded to know what I was doing. Finally I just had to tell her. I went pretty honest about everything I was in that moment."

115.

"...building up inside her for a while because she'd been thinking I was cheating on her. Lucky for her I'm not that kind of guy?"

116.

"...days later made it clear she would leave me if she ever 'discovered' anything else about me. We hit a higher level of trust in some ways. At the same time it was one of those cracks you know will eventually break you. I loved her, I was just on a different planet."

117.

"...came back to the conversation with him, I was still solid in wanting to do the hit myself and he wasn't having it. He said I couldn't live with myself. I'd never sleep again. It would ruin me and it would hurt my family to know a zombie version of me."

118.

"...tried explaining that I'd come up with a strange but simple delivery method. A way that would be somewhat easy but it meant going for everyone rather than just the man I was after. He took a long pause after I unpacked my idea. Finally he just said "You can't do that." It was an odd feeling because I honestly thought he was going to be proud of me for figuring it out the way I did."

119.

"...said he was absolutely doing this himself
and didn't give on it."

120.

"...can't begin to unpack all the moments I've been saved from myself. Basically like luck is my superpower. Times I almost cut fingers off or lost a foot, almost getting busted, near miss accidents on my motorcycle. I actually rode the motorcycle totally illegally for two years and even got pulled over once and the officer says "I must've called in the plate number wrong." instead of ticketing me for no registration, insurance, license, anything. Said I was going slow and he just wanted to make sure I wasn't on pills or drunk."

121.

"...knew I'd let myself go too far. There was no reason to kill the man's wife, and his daughter certainly didn't deserve an early death. I had really lost my mind. I was ready to take all three of them."

122.

"...thought about the final "go" for almost two weeks. Eventually I convinced myself that I didn't care about any of the consequences and wanted to follow through on what I had worked to develop to this point."

123.

"...told him I wanted to go with it. He made
a call to set up his ride and said wait 2 or 3
weeks. In that time, felt like a week later,
the man and his family were gone. They'd
moved out of the state to a near enough city,
but the logistics of setting the whole thing up
again for a new location were beyond my
scope."

124.

"I was more angry than I'd ever been. It was a degree of anger that brought me to tears. I slammed my hands into my kitchen table to the point I thought the table or my hands would break. "

125.

"...don't know what happened, but I've thought about it more than I probably should. In one way the timing of everything unfolding made perfect sense, and in another way I just couldn't make sense of it. He had lived in that house for years and didn't seem like he was going anywhere. At the same time, we live in a cosmos not a chaos and timing is divine."

126.

"When we talked about it he seemed as confused as I was and said maybe it was possible the guy noticed a tail at some point."

127.

"...spent a good amount of time researching every routine move this man made. It was certainly possible to walk up at some point and let him know he needed to leave. He may have seen this as the bigger favor. Saving my future and this guy's life with a simple "Hey you gotta get out of this city". Knowing him, I give this possibility 50/50 odds."

128.

"...have no idea, but really just slowly driving by the guy with a certain look. That's all it would take. You'd get it and be gone."

129.

"...think he got to a point where he didn't want to do it, but if he just walked away he was afraid I'd do it myself. My way really just wasn't cool. Would've been more than my biggest mistake in life, it would have been my own death."

130.

"...such that Arjuna is always free to choose in every moment to walk off the battlefield. The Buddhist route goes something like this. That which is Real is that which exists intrinsically, in itself, independent of other existences. Our existence is dependent on the existence of other phenomena both for the body and the mind. Our bodies are certainly recognized to have no intrinsic existence as they can be busted down into a cycling of atoms. We'd trade them for new ones and feel that we've maintained our true self. Mental experiences in the framework of the human cognition are certainly not what we are either. That would be fundamentally like identifying with 'atomic' bits of mental experience and this is not something we can hold identity with. We identify with a continuity of consciousness, not a series of atomic bits of consciousness. The continuity can only be discussed as any sort of "self" dependent on designators of experiences both mental and physical. We don't believe ourselves to be some unchanging continuity anyway, we believe we can be new and different as we go."

131.

"…as the knower is different from what is known or experienced. So there's no self to be found in states of consciousness or cognitive experiences. There are no labels in any conceptual modeling or language that can be applied. There is no way to tell the guy "you're a warrior so you have to fight in war."

132.

"...because if we say the true experience of the self comes from a process or practices through our actions or meditations then it becomes analyzable into those steps of the process or practices. Again existing dependently, not in itself or intrinsically."

133.

"...keep unpacking it and it's just more emptiness. The material goes empty, then the spacetime itself goes empty, then the concept of empty becomes empty. The emptiness vanishes with the framework for even conceiving 'empty'."

134.

"...then why does it exist at all right? Sure it's not *real,* but it exists, because the 'infinitely singular unchanging eternal oneness' gets bored. It's alone. Being split into fractals makes things much more fun. Our brains are left and right designed to see and understand a unified cosmos and the chaos. Observing this line entertains us."

135.

"Reality, or that which is beyond even the framework for conceiving reality, is boring."

136.

"....think of God as the light and think of the Sun, but it's really about the light of the night. The Universe of light that is revealed to us when it's dark."

137.

"...know what it's like to lose your mind, that's where we really dial in the genius of the human. I'm just saying choose your world and identity constantly, don't crystallize or be someone. Like making the choice with each breath, it's really what's happening anyway. Every dollar votes the economy in a certain direction, every breath is a push in a direction."

138.

"...standing in your chariot on the battlefield. One of them is telling you to kill them all because their spirit will live eternally, and the other one is saying you're not real and this barely exists."

139.

"...sometimes imagine if I'd spent that time doing something else in the world. If I spent three years finding the perfect partner to start a company, or really dove in on some art or a classic car rebuild. Maybe planned to give someone the perfect gift in life rather than planning their death."

140.

"...just wish I had tried to find him again before it wasn't an option. Not in this world, in a different one though right? That's how this works?"

THE

END

www.ingramcontent.com/pod-product-compliance
Lightning Source LLC
Chambersburg PA
CBHW060749180626
46818CB00002B/508